THE
GULF WAR

BY ANITA YASUDA

The Child's World

Published by The Child's World®
1980 Lookout Drive • Mankato, MN 56003-1705
800-599-READ • www.childsworld.com

ACKNOWLEDGMENTS
The Child's World®: Mary Berendes, Publishing Director
Red Line Editorial: Editorial direction
The Design Lab: Design
Amnet: Production
Content Consultant: Ronald Martz, Instructor of History,
University of North Georgia

Photographs ©: Public Domain, cover; iStock/Thinkstock,
4; The Design Lab, 5; Corbis, 6; Marcy Nighswander/AP
Images, 7; AP Images, 9; Greg English/AP Images, 10; Najlah
Feanny/Corbis, 11; Kuna/AP Images, 12; Scott Applewhite/
AP Images, 13 Marty Lederhandler/AP Images, 15; U.S.
Navy, 16; Ron Edmonds/AP Images, 17 (top); Library of
Congress, 17 (bottom); U.S. Army, 18; Defense Imagery, 19,
23; Tech Sgt. Perry Heimer, 20; Tech Sgt. Joe Coleman, 21;
Spencer Weiner/AP Images, 25; Public Domain, 26; Jassim
Mohammed/AP Images, 27; Staff Sgt. Krista M. Foeller, 28

Design Element: Shutterstock Images

ISBN 9781631437137
LCCN 2014945410

Printed in the United States of America
Mankato, MN
November, 2014
PA02243

ABOUT THE AUTHOR

Anita Yasuda is the author of more than 80 books for children. She enjoys writing biographies, books about science and social studies, and chapter books. Anita lives with her family and dog in Huntington Beach, California.

TABLE OF CONTENTS

FIRST NIGHT

★ ★ ★

On January 19, 1991, 12 U.S. warplanes soared into the skies above Saudi Arabia. Their mission was to destroy Iraqi missiles and chemical weapons. The planes were part of Operation Desert Storm. Western and Arab countries had come together to force Iraqi troops from the tiny kingdom of Kuwait. Iraq's President, Saddam Hussein, had taken over Kuwait. He never thought that world leaders would try to stop him.

Colonel David Eberly flew one of the jets. Due to a last-minute schedule change, Eberly had volunteered for the mission. As Eberly and his copilot neared their target, intense flashes of light burst into the sky. It was from anti-aircraft guns. The Iraqis knew Eberly's plane was there. Just before Eberly released his bombs, surface-to-air radar locked onto his aircraft.

Saddam Hussein

UNITED STATES

IRAQ

KUWAIT

Oil wells outside of Kuwait City were set on fire by Hussein's troops.

MEDIA COVERAGE

On August 2, 1990, the Iraqi military invaded Kuwait. An air war against Iraq, led by the United States, began on January 17, 1991. This was the first war with 24-hour media coverage. With the click of a button, people could turn on their televisions and watch live events.

Then he spotted what looked like an oil well blazing into the night sky. But Eberly knew better. It was a surface-to-air missile coming directly for him. Eberly rolled his aircraft to avoid it, and the missile streaked by. But a second missile made contact. A bright white light rocked his plane, ripping it apart. Quickly, Eberly and his copilot ejected.

When Eberly awoke on the cold desert floor, he was surrounded by silence. Suddenly he saw truck lights approaching. They were getting closer. Eberly realized he was being hunted. He worried the sound of his heart might give him away. Luckily, the truck drove away.

Eberly then set off into the darkness. He soon found his copilot. They were alive but hundreds of miles within Iraqi territory. Eberly knew his team was in trouble. He was determined to make sure they kept fighting.

ANOTHER VIEW

Eberly and his copilot survived for three days in the desert. They had no food and little water. Shaking from cold, they found a building to hide in. They thought it was empty, but it was not, and they were captured. Try putting yourself in their position. How would you feel knowing your freedom had just come to an end?

CHAPTER TWO

THE COMING STORM

★ ★ ★

Some of the earliest civilizations have roots in the Middle East. Iraq, once called Mesopotamia, is found here. Over thousands of years, different groups have ruled this area. After World War I (1914–1918), Great Britain and France divided the land. Two of the territories they created were Iraq and Kuwait. The Iraqi government did not agree with these borders. It believed Kuwait belonged to Iraq.

For many years a king ruled Iraq. In 1958, the king and his family were killed. Iraq then became a **republic**. New political parties struggled to control the country. On July 17, 1968, the **Ba'ath Party** came to power. Saddam Hussein belonged to this party.

SADDAM HUSSEIN

Hussein was born in 1937. His family was poor. He had to steal food so they could eat. By 20 years old, Hussein was a member

Saddam Hussein became president of Iraq in 1979.

of the Ba'ath Party. He learned to use fear to get what he
wanted. His work was noticed, and he gained power quickly.
In 1968, Hussein was vice president of Iraq. Eleven years
later, he was in charge of the country.

Hussein ruled Iraq as a **dictator**. He killed or jailed people
who challenged him. In 1980, he began an eight-year war with
Iran. Approximately one million people died. Hussein became
more feared after he used chemical weapons on Iraqi Kurds.

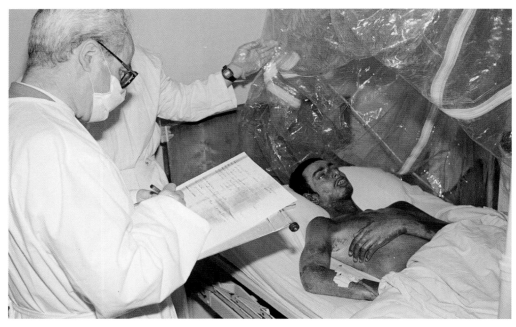

Thousands of Kurds were killed or injured in the chemical attack in 1988.

WAR WITH IRAN

In 1979, Ruhollah Khomeini came to power in Iran. He was a religious leader. His government was based on Islamic law. Hussein worried that Khomeini's ideas may take hold in Iraq, too. Hussein feared this would lead to his downfall. Hussein wanted Iraq to be the more powerful than Iran. For this reason, Hussein went to war with Iran.

The Kurds were the largest minority group in Iraq. They had helped Iran during the war.

KUWAIT

Hussein was determined to rebuild Iraq. But he had borrowed a lot of money for the war against Iran. Most of it came from oil-rich Kuwait. And now Kuwait wanted its money back. On top of this, Hussein faced a big setback. Oil prices were low. Hussein blamed this on Kuwait. In July 1990, he claimed Kuwait was taking oil from Iraqi oil fields. Soon after, Hussein moved Iraqi troops to the Kuwaiti border.

On August 2, 1990, Iraq attacked Kuwait. Iraqi troops and tanks raced over the sand to Kuwait City. People woke to the crackle of gunfire. Then bombs began falling, and walls

Gas prices in 1990 in the United States began to rise because of the conflict in Iraq.

Smoke billows from a building in Kuwait City after a bombing by Iraqi soldiers.

of thick smoke hid buildings. Frantic for news, people called each other. Surprise turned to fear when they learned Iraq had invaded. Most civilians in Kuwait City could not get out. The Iraqi army had set up roadblocks.

Within one day, the Iraqi troops took over the airport and key government buildings. Kuwait's small army was no match for the larger Iraqi force. Kuwait's ruler fled to Saudi Arabia.

Thousands of Kuwaiti people tried to escape in groups across the desert to Saudi Arabia.

ANOTHER VIEW

Kuwait is an oil-rich country. It owns about **6** percent of the world's oil reserves. After the war, Iraq had little money. Kuwait expected Iraq to repay the war debts. If you were a diplomat from another Arab nation, how would you have helped **Kuwait** and **Iraq** reach a deal?

CHAPTER THREE

DEADLINES

raq was now in control of Kuwait. Western and Arab countries reacted strongly to the invasion. Most opposed it. The **United Nations** (UN) called on Iraq to leave Kuwait at once. More and more countries spoke out against Iraq. The United States and the Soviet Union told Hussein to take steps to leave Kuwait. If he did not, they warned him they would take action. This was the first time the United States and the Soviet Union had ever issued a joint statement.

But Hussein did not back down. He said he would turn Kuwait into a "graveyard." The UN approved the use of force to cut off Iraqi trade. Ships from the United States,

GOING TO WAR

Many Arab and Western countries looked for a solution to the crisis. No one wanted a war. U.S. President George H. W. Bush asked for face-to-face talks with Iraq. He hoped a path to peace would be found. But the talks failed. On January 12, 1991, the U.S. Senate voted 52 to 47 to give President Bush the authority to use military force.

The UN Security Council votes to form a blockade on Iraq in 1990. ▶

At one point during Operation Desert Shield, a plane landed at the U.S. base every 11 minutes.

the United Kingdom, Australia, and other countries sailed to the Persian Gulf. They formed a **blockade**. Now Iraq could not export oil.

The UN hoped **sanctions** would lead to peace. Foreign citizens were still trapped in Kuwait. Hussein had begun taking them hostage. He held them at key military sites to discourage the United States from attacking.

THE NEXT MOVE

No one knew what Hussein would do next. This caused fear. Would Hussein's army cross into Saudi Arabia? On August 6, 1990, King Fahd of Saudi Arabia said U.S. troops could set up base in his country. The next day, the first U.S. plane was on its way to the base. U.S. troops had to move far and fast. This mission was called Operation Desert Shield.

President Bush phoned other world leaders and asked for their help in the Persian Gulf.

Meanwhile President George H. W. Bush worked hard to help solve the crisis. He formed a **coalition** of 35 countries. By mid-January there were nearly 700,000 soldiers in Saudi Arabia or on ships in the Persian Gulf. However Iraq was defiant. The UN set a final deadline with Resolution 678. Iraq had to leave Kuwait by midnight on January 15, 1991.

ANOTHER VIEW

President Bush put together a strong coalition of countries against Iraq. Imagine that you have to telephone other world leaders. You must convince them to join you. What would you say to persuade them?

CHAPTER FOUR

THE STORM BEGINS

★ ★ ★

In the early hours of January 17, sirens sounded in Baghdad, Iraq. The city was under attack. **Allied** planes were overhead. They dropped bomb after bomb, pounding Iraqi targets. Light burst across the dark sky. The air war against Iraq had begun. It was called Operation Desert Storm. U.S. General Norman Schwarzkopf Jr. was in charge of the military coalition. The coalition's goal was to force Iraq out of Kuwait.

Norman Schwarzkopf, Jr.

Hussein did not give up easily. He found a way to fight back. Iraq had a large supply of missiles. The next day, alarms went off in Saudi Arabia and Israel. Missiles were headed their way. People ran for cover. Hussein had struck Israel to bring that country into the war. Israel and the surrounding Arab countries had a long history of conflict. If Israel joined the war, Hussein hoped the Arab countries in the coalition would leave the coalition. Hussein's plan did not work. Instead the United States sent missiles to Israel to shoot down Iraqi Scuds.

On January 22, the Iraqi troops set fire to more than 650 Kuwaiti oil wells. The desert filled with oil pools. Large numbers of birds, fish, and sea plants died. The smoke was so thick that it hid the sun. Noon turned into night.

U.S. troops examine a Scud missile that was shot down during Operation Desert Storm.

FOUR-DAY LAND WAR

In the preceding months, the Iraqi troops had been waiting for an attack. General Schwarzkopf had a plan to trap them. He divided his force. He made Hussein think the U.S. soldiers were going to land on the coast. This kept Iraqi troops there.

Instead, on February 24, allied troops stormed into Iraq and Kuwait from Saudi Arabia. The battle was quick. Many of the Iraqi soldiers were new to war and gave up. They were not well prepared.

BAGHDAD BOMBS

Smart bombs were an important part of the allies' air power. Computers and lasers guided them. Still, not all hit the right target. On February 13, two bombs ripped apart a shelter in Baghdad. It was believed to be the Iraqi army's shelter. Sadly, civilians were using it. More than 400 Iraqi civilians were killed.

Another group of U.S. and allied soldiers raced north into the desert. They would take on Hussein's best troops—the Iraqi Republican Guard. The allies took the Iraqi troops by surprise. Their tanks were not facing the right way. However, they did not flee. It was a hard fight, but the allies pushed on and won. After three days of fighting, few allied soldiers had been killed. The Iraqis were not as lucky.

Oil wells burn in the Kuwait desert in 1991. ▶

Destroyed Iraqi vehicles sit abandoned on the "Highway of Death."

On February 26, Iraq announced its troops were leaving Kuwait. Allied aircraft saw thousands of Iraqi tanks and cars fleeing Kuwait. More and more cars kept coming until a road leading to Iraq was jammed. The allies bombed them. Soon burned and torn-up vehicles filled the road. It became known as the "Highway of Death."

FREE KUWAIT

On February 27, allied troops entered Kuwait City. People ran onto the streets to welcome the soldiers. They were free after seven months of Iraqi occupation. Kuwaitis cried tears of relief. Billboards showing Hussein's photograph were set on fire.

Civilians and military members celebrate Iraqi troops leaving Kuwait City.

During the Gulf War, about 150,000 Iraqi soldiers left their positions. Many others surrendered to coalition forces in large numbers. Many Iraqi soldiers were poorly trained and sometimes were not given food for days by their leaders. If you were an Iraqi soldier, what would you have done?

CHAPTER FIVE

END TO WAR

★ ★ ★

Iraq's army, the fourth largest in the world, had been defeated. On February 28, President Bush called for a cease-fire. Iraq agreed to it. Iraq also promised to release all prisoners of war. Within days, U.S. troops began to leave the Middle East. In their place came a UN peacekeeping force.

Back in the United States, people waved flags and held parades for the returning troops. Americans were proud of them. General Schwarzkopf called the soldiers heroes. Of the 500,000 U.S. soldiers sent to the Gulf War, 148 soldiers died in battle. Another 145 died from other causes. The Iraqis had 60,000 to 100,000 soldiers killed or wounded.

WAR'S END

The war was over. But Hussein would show he was still powerful. Soon after the war, two groups rose up against him.

Americans were happy it had been a short war. ▶

Many countries, including Germany, helped with Operation Provide Comfort in 1991.

They were the Marsh Arabs in the south of Iraq and the Kurds in the north. Hussein's forces crushed the revolts. They wiped out Marsh villages.

In the north, 2 million Kurds fled their homes. Hussein's men gunned many people down. The Kurds looked for places to hide in the mountains. With little food or water, many died. On April 6, 1991, the United States began Operation Provide Comfort. Many countries helped out. Camps were built for more than 180,000 **refugees**. Planes dropped first-aid supplies to the refugees.

SANCTIONS

After the Gulf War ended, UN inspections began. The UN wanted to find all of Iraq's chemical weapons. Hussein had already used chemical weapons on his own people. It was thought he would not hesitate to do it again. The UN felt it would be safe to lift the sanctions after inspections. The sanctions were very hard on the Iraqi people. They were going without food. The UN let Iraq sell its oil to pay for food and medicine.

An Iraqi woman carries her family's monthly food rations. The UN sanctions made life difficult for Iraqi people.

A bomber plane is prepared for Operation Desert Fox.

GULF WAR SYNDROME

After the Gulf War, some soldiers began having health problems. They had constant pain, rashes, and headaches. The illness was called Gulf War Syndrome. Troops were given shots and pills to protect them from the chemical weapons Hussein was using. Some experts think these shots and pills were to blame.

However, Hussein made it very difficult for UN inspectors to do their jobs. UN helicopters were stopped from taking off. Inspectors could not enter all suspected weapon sites. This meant the sanctions stayed in place.

In October 1998, Iraq still would not let UN inspectors do their jobs. In response, the United States and the United Kingdom began Operation Desert Fox on December 16. More than 100 Iraqi targets were bombed.

Hussein ruled Iraq until 2003. This is when the United States and the United Kingdom sent forces to the Persian Gulf again, in a different conflict. Hussein's rule finally ended after he was found in a hiding place. The Iraqi government **prosecuted** and killed Hussein. Most Iraqis welcomed the change in power, but peace did not come. Instead many groups began to fight for control of Iraq. U.S. troops stayed in Iraq until December 18, 2011.

ANOTHER VIEW

In June 1991, UN weapon inspections began. Inspectors believed Iraq might have been hiding weapons of mass destruction. Their suspicions grew when Iraq stopped UN inspections. Imagine you were one of these inspectors. What would you have thought when your team was not allowed into a site?

TIMELINE

August 2, 1990	Iraqi troops invade Kuwait.
August 6, 1990	King Fahd of Kuwait asks the United States to help.
August 7, 1990	Operation Desert Shield begins with the first U.S. troops arriving in Saudi Arabia.
November 29, 1990	UN Security Council writes Resolution 678 to make Iraqi forces leave Kuwait.
January 12, 1991	Congress authorizes the use of force in the Persian Gulf.
January 17, 1991	Operation Desert Storm begins with air attacks on Baghdad.
January 19, 1991	Iraq first fires Scud missiles at Israel.
January 22, 1991	Iraq begins blowing up oil wells in Kuwait.
February 24, 1991	Coalition forces launch major ground attack on Iraqi forces in Kuwait and Iraq.
February 28, 1991	A cease-fire of the war begins.
April 11, 1991	The Gulf War officially comes to an end.

GLOSSARY

Allied (AL-ide) Allied means to be joined in an alliance. Allied countries fought together in the Gulf War.

Ba'ath Party (BAH-ahth PAR-tee) The Ba'ath Party is a socialist group of some Arab countries. Saddam Hussein belonged to the Ba'ath Party.

blockade (blok-ADE) A blockade stops people or supplies from entering or leaving a country, especially during war. The United Nations placed a blockade on Iraq's oil exports.

coalition (koh-uh-LISH-un) A coalition is a group of countries that join together for a common goal. President George H. W. Bush formed a coalition of 35 countries during the Gulf War.

dictator (DIK-tay-tur) A dictator is a person who rules a country with absolute authority and often in a cruel way. Saddam Hussein ruled Iraq as a dictator.

prosecuted (PROSS-uh-kyoo-ted) To be prosecuted is to have a trial held against you to see if you are guilty. The Iraqi government prosecuted Saddam Hussein.

refugees (ref-yuh-JEES) Refugees are people forced to leave their country because of war or other threats. Operation Provide Comfort provided supplies for refugees.

republic (ri-PUHB-lik) A republic is a country governed by an elected president and representatives. Iraq became a republic in 1958.

sanctions (SANGK-shuhns) Sanctions are actions taken to enforce laws or rules. The United Nations enforced sanctions on Iraq.

United Nations (yoo-NITED NAY-shuhns) The United Nations is a political organization of 51 countries established in 1945. The United Nations asked Iraq to leave Kuwait during the Gulf War.

TO LEARN MORE

BOOKS

Hossell, Karen Price. *The Persian Gulf War*. Clermont, FL: Paw Prints Publishing, 2008.

Wingate, Brian. *Saddam Hussein*. New York: Rosen Publishing, 2004.

WEB SITES

Visit our Web site for links about the Gulf War: **childsworld.com/links**

Note to Parents, Teachers, and Librarians: We routinely verify our Web links to make sure they are safe and active sites. So encourage your readers to check them out!

INDEX